GW00402335

CONTENTS

Pedigree®

Published 2009.
Published by Pedigree Books Limited, Beech Hill House,
Walnut Gardens, Exeter, Devon EX4 4DH.

© 2009 Lucasfilm Ltd.
All rights reserved. Used under authorization.

£5.99

VILLAINS

WEAPONARY DESIGN STATION

ARMOUR

little droid

Jungle warrior

Storm trooper

bounty Hunter

USING THESE IMAGES AS INSPIRATION, IT IS YOUR MISSION TO DESIGN A SUIT OF ARMOUR AND A WEAPON.

WEAPON

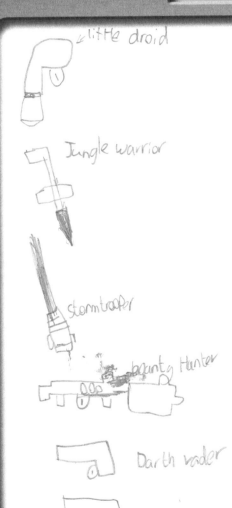

little droid

Jungle warrior

stormtrooper

bounty Hunter

Darth vader

WORD SEARCH

THERE ARE WORDS THAT ARE SO POWERFUL, THEY ECHO AROUND THE GALAXY AND EVEN DOWN THROUGH TIME. CAN YOU FIND ALL THE POWERFUL WORDS THAT ARE LURKING IN THIS GALACTIC GRID? GIVE YOURSELF A GOLD STAR IF YOU FIND EVERY SINGLE ONE!

Q	W	H	E	R	T	Y	U	R	I	O	E	P	A	S	D	F	G	C
A	S	D	T	F	G	H	A	J	K	L	M	L	Z	X	C	V	O	I
F	V	B	N	I	N	T	M	Q	A	Z	P	W	S	X	E	R	D	L
D	E	C	R	F	S	V	B	G	T	Y	I	V	B	G	U	T	Y	B
Y	H	T	N	H	M	J	P	I	H	S	R	A	T	S	U	I	O	U
L	P	M	T	N	B	V	M	C	X	Z	E	A	C	S	D	A	F	P
G	H	A	J	K	L	P	O	U	I	U	Y	A	T	R	D	E	W	E
Q	E	M	A	S	D	F	G	H	S	J	N	K	L	O	P	O	C	R
D	O	I	E	R	O	T	Y	S	N	T	P	O	Y	I	U	Y	L	E
E	W	R	Q	L	K	B	J	H	G	F	A	D	S	A	A	Z	O	X
X	C	R	V	B	N	B	I	G	R	Y	S	F	D	D	I	R	N	U
P	O	E	U	Y	O	S	A	W	E	R	V	X	A	N	D	M	E	J
Q	W	T	E	R	C	T	Y	U	A	I	O	P	J	R	E	G	S	D
T	T	U	H	G	L	G	F	A	R	N	A	X	O	E	J	A	D	F
B	V	O	O	B	A	N	X	D	O	E	L	I	L	G	T	E	D	C
R	T	Y	U	I	F	O	P	L	K	J	D	H	G	E	F	D	S	A
T	N	M	D	S	E	R	T	Y	U	S	J	A	F	D	C	C	V	W
I	J	B	F	E	S	Z	X	D	F	T	Y	U	V	I	O	R	L	N
S	K	Y	W	A	L	K	E	R	U	R	V	S	F	Q	W	E	O	S
Z	X	C	G	H	J	U	I	O	W	E	R	T	Y	U	I	O	P	F

- ☐ CLONES
- ☐ CORUSCANT
- ☐ FORCE
- ☐ DROIDS
- ☐ EMPIRE
- ☐ FALCON
- ☐ FETT
- ☐ DEATH STAR
- ☐ REPUBLIC
- ☐ JEDI
- ☐ MUSTAFAR
- ☐ NABOO
- ☐ OBI-WAN
- ☐ OUTER RIM
- ☐ HUTT
- ☐ SITH
- ☐ SKYWALKER
- ☐ STARSHIP
- ☐ VADER
- ☐ YODA

TRUE OR FALSE?

WHICH OF THE STATEMENTS BELOW IS TRUE? CAN YOU PINPOINT THE TRUTH LIKE OBI-WAN KENOBI, OR ARE YOU AS EASILY DECEIVED AS JAR JAR BINKS?

		TRUE	FALSE
1.	ADMIRAL ACKBAR IS THE COMMANDER OF THE ALLIANCE FLEET.	☐	☐
2.	ANAKIN SKYWALKER'S NICKNAME IS 'THE HERO WITH NO FEAR'.	☐	☐
3.	BIGGS DARKLIGHTER WAS ONCE LUKE SKYWALKER'S BEST FRIEND.	☐	☐
4.	BOSS NASS IS A BOUNTY HUNTER.	☐	☐
5.	BOSSK IS A BOUNTY HUNTER.	☐	☐
6.	C-3PO WAS BUILT BY ANAKIN SKYWALKER.	☐	☐
7.	DEXTER JETTSTER IS A HUTT GANGSTER.	☐	☐
8.	GRAND MOFF TARKIN'S HOME PLANET IS ERIADU.	☐	☐
9.	GREEDO DIED WHEN HE FELL IN THE PIT OF CARKOON.	☐	☐
10.	HAN SOLO BECAME THE SITH LORD DARTH VADER.	☐	☐
11.	NEIMOIDIANS ARE KNOWN FOR BEING COWARDLY AND MONEY-LOVING.	☐	☐
12.	MASTER YODA IS LUKE SKYWALKER'S FATHER.	☐	☐
13.	MON MOTHMA IS AN ALIEN IN THE SHAPE OF A GIANT MOTH.	☐	☐
14.	ONE OF THE HEROES OF THE REBEL ALLIANCE IS HAN SOLO.	☐	☐
15.	PADMÉ AMIDALA BECAME A SENATOR AFTER SHE WAS QUEEN OF NABOO.	☐	☐
16.	R2-D2 IS A PROTOCOL DROID.	☐	☐
17.	SHMI SKYWALKER IS A RICH AND POWERFUL HUTT.	☐	☐
18.	OBI-WAN KENOBI WAS PADAWAN TO QUI-GON JINN.	☐	☐
19.	SUPREME CHANCELLOR VALORUM ORGANISED THE REBEL ALLIANCE.	☐	☐
20.	WATTO IS A KIND-HEARTED EWOK WHO SAVED PRINCESS LEIA'S LIFE.	☐	☐

11

STARSHIP STATISTICS
SECTION 1

B-WING STARFIGHTER
TYPE: Starfighter
AFFILIATION: Rebel Alliance
SIZE: 16.9m tall, 4.7m long
WEAPONS: Laser cannon, proton torpedoes, light ion cannons, auto blasters

DROID TRI-FIGHTER
TYPE: Starfighter
AFFILIATION: Confederacy of Independent Systems, Trade Federation
SIZE: 5.4m long
WEAPONS: Laser cannons, light laser cannons, buzz-droid missile launcher

IMPERIAL LAMBDA-CLASS SHUTTLE
TYPE: Multi-purpose shuttle
AFFILIATION: Empire
SIZE: 20m long
WEAPONS: Double blaster cannons, double laser cannons, light armour plating, deflector shield generators

IMPERIAL STAR DESTROYER
TYPE: Battle starcruiser *Imperator*-class
AFFILIATION: Empire
SIZE: 1,600m long
WEAPONS: Turbolaser batteries, ion cannons, tractor beam projectors

JEDI STARFIGHTER
TYPE: Delta-7 *Aethersprite* light interceptor
AFFILIATION: Jedi
SIZE: 8m long. 3.92m widest, 1.44m tall
WEAPONS: Dual laser cannons

MILLENNIUM FALCON
TYPE: YT-1300 stock light freighter
AFFILIATION: Smuggling, Rebel Alliance
SIZE: 26.7m long, 20m wide, 5m tall
WEAPONS: Quad laser cannons, concussion missile tubes, blaster cannon

NABOO N-1 STARFIGHTER
TYPE: N-1 Royal starfighter
AFFILIATION: The Naboo
SIZE: 11m long
WEAPONS: Twin laser cannons, proton torpedoes

NABOO ROYAL STARSHIP
TYPE: J-Type 327 Nubian Ship
AFFILIATION: The Naboo
SIZE: 76m long
WEAPONS: None

NABOO ROYAL CRUISER
TYPE: J-type diplomatic barge
AFFILIATION: The Naboo
SIZE: 39m long, 91m wide, 6.8m tall
WEAPONS: None

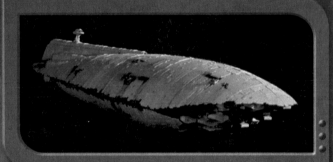

REBEL MEDIUM TRANSPORT
TYPE: GR-75 medium transport
AFFILIATION: Rebel Alliance
SIZE: 90m long
WEAPONS: Twin laser cannons

REPUBLIC ASSAULT SHIP
TYPE: *Acclamator*-class transport
AFFILIATION: Galactic Republic
SIZE: 752m long, 460m wide, 200m tall
WEAPONS: Quad turbolaser turrets, laser cannons,
missile/torpedo launch tubes

ARCHIVE FILES
PLANET PROFILES: CORUSCANT

SITTING AT THE HEART OF THE GALAXY, CORUSCANT IS A COLD WORLD WITH A DIM, WHITE SUN. ACCORDING TO STANDARD NAVIGATION CHARTS, IT IS THE CENTRE OF THE UNIVERSE. IT IS AT THE MEETING POINT OF SEVERAL HYPER-ROUTES, INCLUDING THE MARTIAL CROSS, THE SHAWKEN SPUR, THE KOROS TRUNK LINE, THE METELLOS TRADE ROUTE, THE PERLEMIAN TRADE ROUTE, AND THE CORELLIAN RUN.

Pronunciation: COR-uhh-saant	**Terrain:** Urban
Other names: Jewel of the Core Worlds, Imperial Centre, The Abyss	**Native Species:** Humans, corridor ghouls, hawk-bats, spider-roaches, armoured rats, duracrete worms, shadow-barnacles, granite slugs, Cthon, sewer rats
Size: 12,240km diameter	**Species Mix:** 68% human, 32% other
Distance from core: 10,000 light years	**Population:** 1 trillion Coruscanti
Suns: 1	**Capital City:** Galactic City
Moons: 4	**Places of Interest:** Jedi Temple, Galactic Senate Chamber, Imperial Palace, Monument Plaza, Senate Chambers, Crimson Corridor, Westport, Eastport, Dexter's Diner, Outlander Club, University of Coruscant, Golden Cuff, Dewback Inn, Tusken Oasis
Surface Water: 29% (ice caps)	
Composition: Molten core with rocky mantle and silicate rock crust	
Length of Day: 24 standard hours	
Climate: Temperate and controlled	

Almost every area of the planet is inhabited. It is covered in huge, sprawling cities that reach up to 6,000 metres into the atmosphere. Coruscant's busy skylanes are crowded with starships day and night.

Coruscant is divided into quadrants, which are often given unofficial names. For example, quadrant H-46 is better known as Sah'c Town, after the family who owns most of it.

The city foundations have been in place since the early days of the Republic, but construction droids work day and night to repair structures or build new ones. All buildings are climate-controlled and their windows reflect sunlight. The planet's heat is controlled by thousands of reactive dampers.

Coruscant is dominated by humans, but a few animals share the world. Kitelike hawk-bats live in artificial canyons below the surface, feeding on granite slugs. Four-legged corridor ghouls also lurk beneath the surface, along with a variety of other life-forms.

HISTORY FILES
BATTLE OF NABOO

THE BATTLE OF NABOO WAS THE CONFLICT THAT UNITED THE NABOO AND GUNGANS AGAINST THE TRADE FEDERATION. IT BEGAN WHEN THE TRADE FEDERATION INVADED THE PEACEFUL PLANET OF NABOO AS A PROTEST AGAINST THE TAXATION OF TRADE ROUTES. QUEEN AMIDALA ESCAPED AND ASKED THE GALACTIC SENATE FOR HELP, BUT THEY REFUSED TO ACT IMMEDIATELY.

Worried for her people, the Queen returned home with Jedi Master Qui-Gon Jinn, his apprentice Obi-Wan Kenobi and a young boy named Anakin Skywalker. With the help of Gungan of Jar Jar Binks, the Queen united with Boss Nass, ruler of the Gungans. Together, they prepared to stand against their common enemy.

Battle Strategy
Queen Amidala and her allies concocted a clever plan, splitting into groups to achieve their goal. The Gungans distracted the Trade Federation droid army with a full-scale battle, while the Naboo and the Jedi broke into the Royal Palace.

In the palace, the Jedi fought the Sith warrior Darth Maul while Queen Amidala and her soldiers searched for Nute Gunray, the Trade Federation's viceroy.

At the same time, Naboo's Bravo Flight launched an attack on the droid control ship. Little Anakin Skywalker was hiding in one of the Naboo starfighters, and he became entangled in the space battle.

FACTS AND FIGURES

The invasion force consisted of 33 large transports and 342 battle tanks.

The Trade Federation army included deadly droid starfighters, unstoppable transports (MTTs), and devastating tanks (AATs).

Cargo vessels were converted to serve as battleships.

MULTI TROOP TRANSPORTS (MTTs)

SIZE: 31m long, 13m tall
WEAPONS: 4 anti-personnel blasters
TOP SPEED: 35 kph
CREW: 2 pilot droids, 2 additional battle droids
PASSENGERS: 112 battle droids
FLIGHT CEILING: 4m

SARMOURED ASSAULT TANKS (AATs)

SIZE: 9.75m long
WEAPONS: Primary turret laser cannon, twin lateral range-finding lasers, twin lateral anti-personnel lasers, 6 energy shell projectile launchers
TOP SPEED: 55 kph
CREW: 4 battle droids

Gungan Glory

The Gungan army had only primitive weapons, but their mission was not to defeat the Trade Federation. Instead, their troop movements were designed to draw the Trade Federation army away from the city.

The plan worked well. As soon as the Gungans emerged from the swamps, the Trade Federation sent dozens of MTTs, AATs and STAPs to the battlefield. Each MTT was protected by at least five AATs, which targeted the Gungan shield generators. The Gungans were outnumbered and overcome, but their heroic 'distraction' allowed the Queen's forces to break into the Royal Palace.

A Heavy Price

The Battle of Naboo took its toll on the freedom fighters. Darth Maul murdered Qui-Gon Jinn, but was slain by Obi-Wan Kenobi. The Gungans fought bravely but were overwhelmed by battle droids and droidekas. Queen Amidala captured Nute Gunray, but they were trapped in the throne room.

Bold Bravo Pilots

Bravo Flight pilots seized their Naboo N-1 starfighters and launched an attack against the Trade Federation's droid control ship. The N-1 was not an assault fighter, but the Bravo Flight pilots used exceptional skill to survive. They flew dangerously close to the droid control ship so that its turbolasers could not target them. When they were attacked by droid starfighters, the Naboo pilots kept changing their attack patterns to overload the droids' tactical processors.

Young Hero

Anakin Skywalker flew an N-1 starfighter into the droid battleship's main hangar. He used the N-1's proton torpedoes to destroy the droid control ship's main reactor, which exploded the ship and ended the invasion.

EXERCISE

Using the words opposite, complete the three major results of the battle of Naboo.

1. .... and his lieutenant, ..., were taken into Republic custody.
2. The .... and .... formed a lasting peace.
3. .... became ....'s Padawan.

- Anakin Skywalker
- Gungans
- Naboo
- Nute Gunray
- Obi-Wan Kenobi
- Rune Haako

IDENTITY PARADE

1

2

3
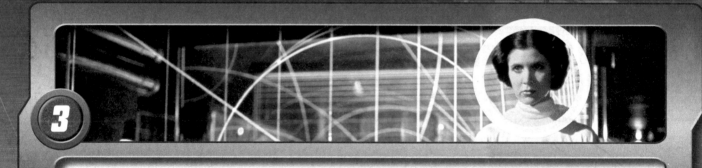

4

5

6

7

8

ARCHIVE FILES
PLANET PROFILES: KAMINO

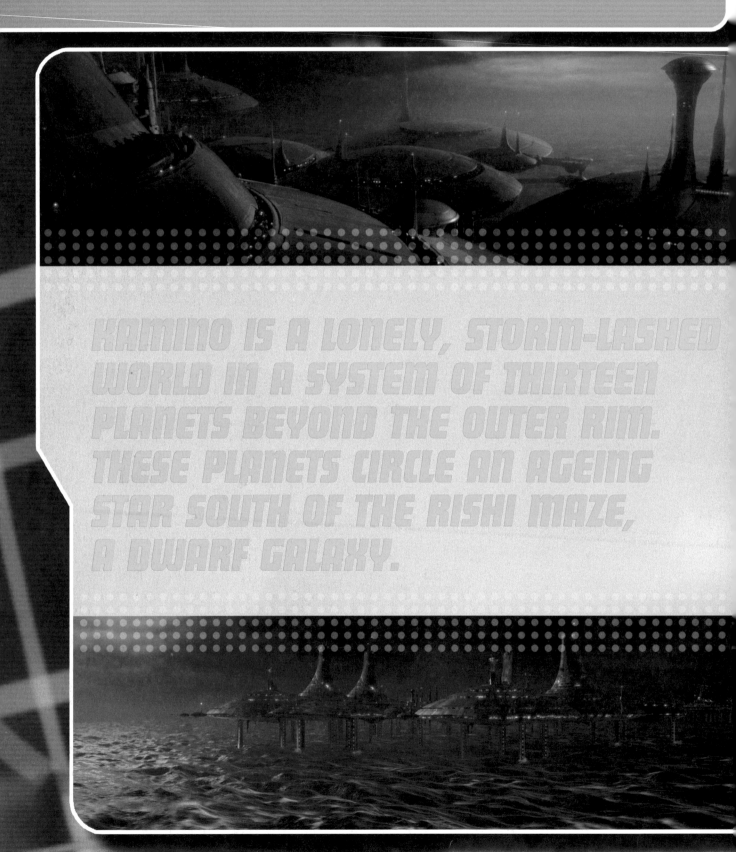

KAMINO IS A LONELY, STORM-LASHED WORLD IN A SYSTEM OF THIRTEEN PLANETS BEYOND THE OUTER RIM. THESE PLANETS CIRCLE AN AGEING STAR SOUTH OF THE RISHI MAZE, A DWARF GALAXY.

Pronunciation: kuh-MEE-noe
Size: 19,270km diameter
Distance from core: 70,000 light years
Suns: 1
Moons: 3
Surface water: 100%

Composition: Molten core with rocky mantle and silicate rock crust
Climate: Rainstorms
Terrain: Ocean
Native Species: Aiwhas, rollerfish, sea-mice, fanteels
Population: 1 billion Kaminoans
Places of Interest: Tipoca City, clone factory

Because of climate change, the planet is now one huge ocean. Kamino once had large areas of land, but melting glaciers made all land sink beneath the waves. Powerful storms rage endlessly and the seas are full of predators. The Kaminoan stilt cities rise above the water, built to withstand the storms.

Kamino's most prized export is clones, and the Kaminoans trade their advanced cloning knowledge for vital raw materials. They are said to be the best cloners in the galaxy, and the Grand Army of the Republic was hatched, grown and trained at the facilities on Kamino. To supply the army with armour and transport, the Kaminoans partnered with the Rothana system to develop advanced combat machinery.

As well as creating clones, the Kaminoans can produce specialised weapons and missiles for clients. Poisonous kyberdarts and saberdarts come from Kamino. The Kaminoans' knowledge of genetic engineering and xenobiology has enabled them to develop biotoxins that kill in seconds.

A Kamino saberdart was used by Jango Fett to kill Zam Wesell. When Obi-Wan took the toxic, fork-shaped dart to the Jedi Temple analysis rooms, the SP-4 droids were unable to identify it. They suggested that a lone warrior made it. However, Obi-Wan's old friend Dexter Jettster knew better, and he told the Jedi about Kamino.

After the Clone Wars, some Kaminoans tried to create a clone army to fight against the Empire. Ten years after the defeat of the Jedi, these clones started an uprising, but were crushed by the 501st Legion of stormtroopers, led by Boba Fett.

MACHINE DESIGN STATION

AT-AT

SIZE: 15.5m tall, 20.6m long   TOP SPEED: 60 kph
CREW: 3   PASSENGERS: 40   CARGO: 5 speeder bikes
WEAPONS: 2 heavy laser cannons, 2 medium blasters

USE THIS GRID DESIGN BLUEPRINT OF
AN AT-AT (ALL TERRAIN ARMOURED
TRANSPORT) TO CREATE YOUR OWN
VERSION OF THE IMPOSING IMPERIAL
WALKER.

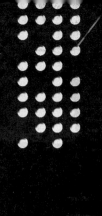

AT-AT

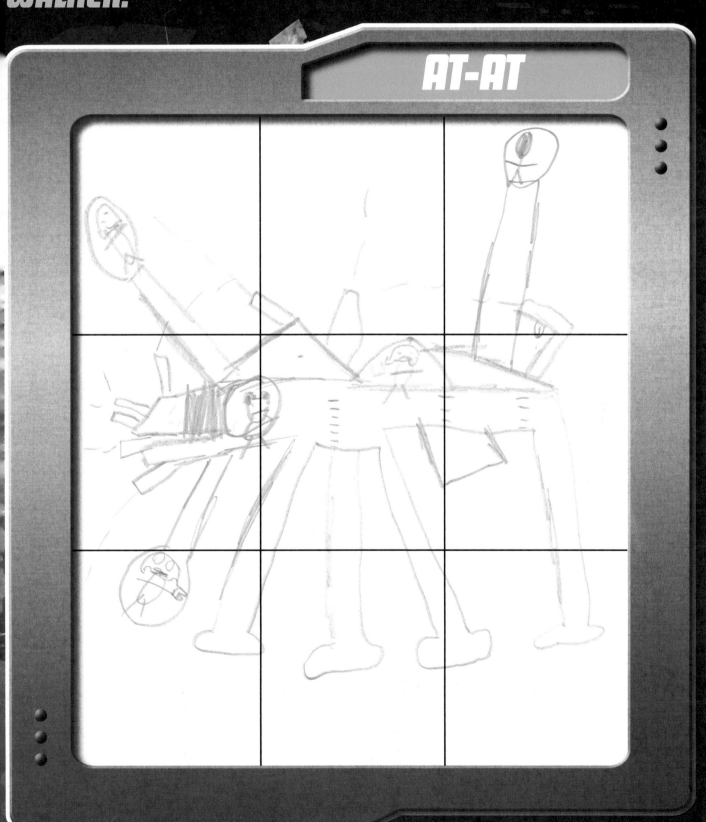

HISTORY FILES
BATTLE OF GEONOSIS

IN THE YEARS LEADING UP TO THE CLONE WARS, COUNT DOOKU FORMED A SEPARATIST MOVEMENT WITH VARIOUS GROUPS WHO WERE UNHAPPY WITH THE GALACTIC REPUBLIC. THESE DISSATISFIED GROUPS OFFICIALLY FOUNDED THE CONFEDERACY OF INDEPENDENT SYSTEMS AT A MEETING ON GEONOSIS, WHERE FOUNDRIES HAD PRODUCED WEAPONS AND VEHICLES READY FOR WAR.

Meanwhile, the Republic had discovered a clone army on Kamino. Fearing the separatists, the Republic assumed control of the clone army and launched an invasion on Geonosis.

Battle Strategy
The Republic planned the invasion as a sudden attack that would destroy the Confederacy before it could gain more power. After breaking through the atmosphere with huge military assault ships, the Republic sent a fleet of gunships to the planet's surface. The transports carried thousands of clone troopers and dozens of AT-TE walkers. The army advanced on the Geonosian arena, where a Jedi strike team was surrounded, then attacked the battle droid foundries.

REPUBLIC FORCES FIGURES

Clone trooper: 192,000 deployed in battle
LAAT/i gunship: 1,600 deployed in battle
LAAT/c (AT-TE carrier): 400 deployed in battle
AT-TE: 2,160 deployed in battle
SPHA-T: 100 deployed in battle
Assault ship: 12 deployed in battle

SEPARATIST FORCES FIGURES

Battle droid: 1,000,000 deployed in battle
Super battle droid: 100,000 deployed in battle
Droideka: 3,000 deployed in battle
Dwarf spider droid: 15,000 deployed in battle
Sonic cannon: 4 deployed in arena
Hailfire droid: 4,100 deployed in battle
Homing spider droid: 7,500 deployed in battle
Techno Union starship: 286 deployed in battle (169 escaped)
Commerce Guild starship: 41 deployed in battle (36 escaped)
Trade Federation core ship: 60 deployed in battle (46 escaped)

Stand-off

The Confederacy and its allies refused to surrender. Geonosian starfighters tried to stop the clone troopers, but the AT-TE walkers, gunships, and a handful of Jedi starfighters kept them at bay.

Tank droids, hailfire units, and homing droids managed to slow down the clone army, but they could not be stopped completely.

The Advantage of Speed

The Jedi commanders began spreading their forces to surround the slow-moving droids. Reconnaissance troopers raced across the battlefield on speeder bikes, gathering vital information about enemy troop movements and capabilities.

The remaining Jedi were airlifted to safety, while the battle continued on the ground between troops and vehicles. When the Confederacy leaders realised that the Republic was going to win the battle, they tried to send their core ships to safety. These ships contained battle droids, weapons and vehicles. Every single ship was like a small army. Destroying them became a priority.

Victory

The heavy artillery units had advanced turbolasers which managed to bring down several of the core ships, crippling the Confederacy's army.

ALL TERRAIN TACTICAL ENFORCER WALKERS (AT-TEs)

SIZE: 13.2m long (excluding guns), 7.41m tall (with turret)
WEAPONS: 6 anti-personnel laser cannon turrets, 1 heavy projectile cannon
TOP SPEED: 60 kph
CREW: 1 pilot, 1 spotter, 4 gunner/support crew, 1 exterior gunner
PASSENGERS: 20 clone troopers, 1IM-6 Battlefield Medical Droid

EXERCISE

Using the words opposite, complete this summary of the battle of Geonosis.

The .... resulted in the deaths of many .... and legions of .... troopers. Even though the .... won the battle, they made the .... more determined to continue. The .... had begun.

Battle of Geonosis
clone
Clone Wars
Jedi
Republic
Separatists

THE RESCUE OF PRINCESS LEIA

IT WAS ON BOARD THE DEATH STAR ITSELF THAT THREE HEROES OF THE REBEL ALLIANCE CAME TOGETHER FOR THE FIRST TIME. LUKE SKYWALKER HAD JOURNEYED ACROSS THE STARS AFTER SEEING A HOLOGRAM OF THE BEAUTIFUL PRINCESS LEIA, WITH THE HELP OF THE SMUGGLER HAN SOLO. WHEN LUKE REALISED THAT THE PRINCESS WAS ON BOARD THE DEATH STAR, NOTHING COULD PREVENT HIM FROM TRYING TO RESCUE HER . . .

Luke stared at the dazzling young princess, amazed by her beauty.
"I'm Luke Skywalker," he stammered.
"I'm here to rescue you."

Together they raced out of the cell into the hallway, only to see Han Solo and Chewbacca running towards them. Behind them, Imperial troops were firing through smoke and flame.

"Can't get out that way," said Han.
"Looks like you managed to cut off our only escape route," Leia commented.
"Maybe you'd like it back in your cell, Your Highness," Han snapped, sounding a little stressed.

Luke reached for his comlink transmitter as they exchanged fire with the oncoming stormtroopers.
"See-Threepio!" he cried.
"Are there any other ways out of the cell bay?"

In the control tower, Threepio yelled into the comlink transmitter.
"All systems have been alerted to your presence, sir!" he reported. "The main entrance seems to be the only way in or out; all other information on your level is restricted."

Luke and Leia crouched together in an alcove as Han and Chewbacca tried to keep the stormtroopers at the far end of the hallway. Smoke from the laserfire filled the narrow corridor.

"There isn't any other way out," Luke declared.
"I can't hold them off forever!" retorted Han. "Now what?"

"This is some rescue," Leia remarked, glaring at Han. "When you came in here, didn't you have a plan for getting out?"
"He's the brains, sweetheart," said Han.

Leia gave them both an exasperated look and grabbed Luke's gun. She fired at a small grate in the wall next to Han, almost frying him.

"What the hell are you doing?" Han yelled.

"Somebody has to save our skins!" Leia replied.
"Into the garbage chute, fly boy."
She jumped through the narrow grate as Han and Chewbacca stared in amazement.

Chewbacca sniffed the garbage chute and spoke. Only Han understood him, and Han was not impressed.
"Get in there, you big furry oaf!" Han ordered. "I don't care what you smell! Get in there and don't worry about it!"

He gave the complaining Wookiee a kick and Chewbacca disappeared through the tiny opening. Luke and Han continued firing.

"Wonderful girl!" Han exclaimed, thinking of the Princess. "Either I'm going to kill her or I'm beginning to like her. Get in there!

Luke didn't like the sound of that, but there was no time to talk about it. He ducked laserfire and jumped into the darkness.

Han fired off a couple of quick blasts to create a smokey cover, then slid into the chute and was gone. They were all safe . . . for now.

QUIZZICAL

TEST YOUR KNOWLEDGE OF GALACTIC HISTORY!

Identify these aliens by name and species.

 **a.**

 **b.**

 **c.**

1

2 Tauntauns are starfighters, true or false?

3 What navigational system did Luke Skywalker use to destroy the Death Star at the Battle of Yavin?

4 Why did Luke Skywalker agree to travel with Obi-Wan Kenobi?

5 Name the Chosen One.

6 Where was the first battle of the Clone Wars?

7 Who was Princess Leia's grandmother?

8 Why did Anakin Skywalker become Darth Vader?

9 On which planet was Boba Fett born?

10 Who killed Qui-Gon Jinn?

11 When was the Emperor's face scarred?

12 Where was Anakin Skywalker's funeral?

13 Who did General Grievous kidnap shortly before the end of the Clone Wars?

14 What were Padmé Amidala's last words?

15 Why did Luke Skywalker leave Master Yoda before his training was complete?

16 Who did Jango Fett hire to assassinate Padmé Amidala?

17 Where did Han Solo meet Obi-Wan Kenobi?

18 What is a Jedi not allowed to do?

19 Use your stickers to identify the owner of each of these weapons.

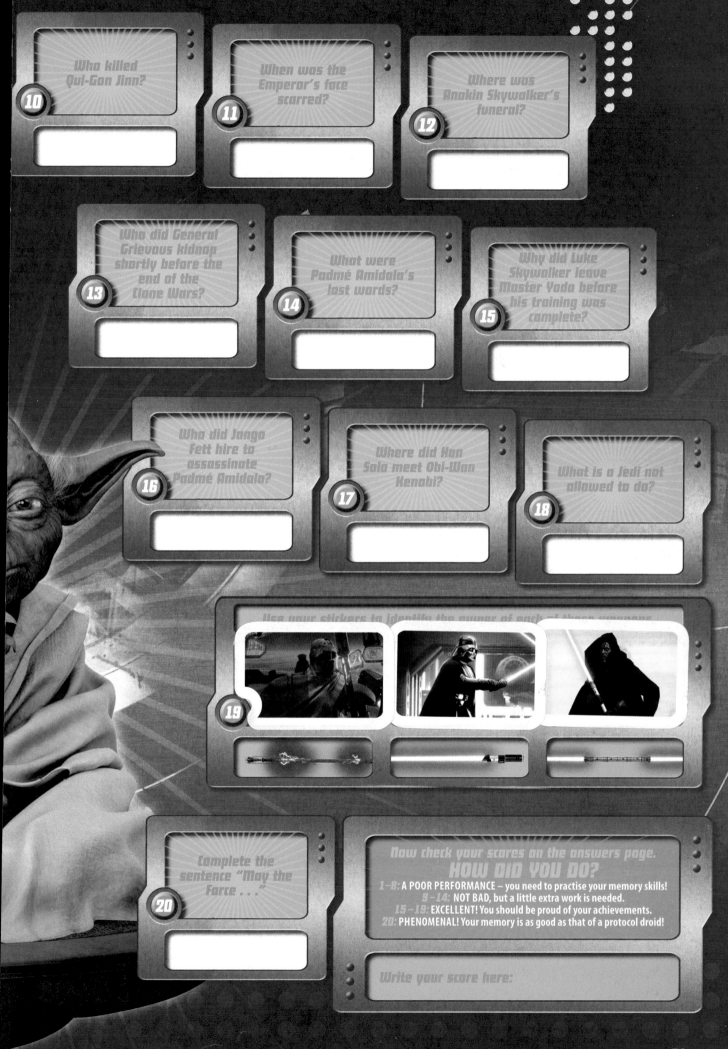

20 Complete the sentence "May the Force . . ."

Now check your scores on the answers page.
HOW DID YOU DO?
1–8: A POOR PERFORMANCE – you need to practise your memory skills!
9–14: NOT BAD, but a little extra work is needed.
15–19: EXCELLENT! You should be proud of your achievements.
20: PHENOMENAL! Your memory is as good as that of a protocol droid!

Write your score here:

THE ALIENS OF MOS EISLEY CANTINA

?

A

SPECIES: Abyssin
HOMEWORLD: Byss
SIZE: 2m tall
EYES: 1

This alien is a cyclops desert dweller. He is self-regenerating, aggressive and completely fearless. Don't call him a 'Monoc' or you will start a fight! He is a mercenary and general thug, and spends a lot of time in the Outer Rim Territories.

?

D

SPECIES: Talz
HOMEWORLD: Alzoc III
SIZE: 2.1m tall
EYES: 4
SKIN COLOUR: Grey
HAIR COLOUR: White

This alien grew up in the streets of Mos Eisley and made a living doing odd jobs and begging. He and his best friend Kabe once lived on the credits that Kabe stole. He made a little money himself by selling information.

WHEN LUKE SKYWALKER ARRIVED AT MOS EISLEY CANTINA WITH OBI-WAN KENOBI, HE HAD NO IDEA OF THE DANGEROUS AND EXCITING ADVENTURES THAT WERE AHEAD OF HIM. HE WAS BEWILDERED BY THE VARIETY OF ALIENS IN THE CANTINA. CAN YOU IDENTIFY THEM ALL FROM THEIR DESCRIPTIONS? USE YOUR KNOWLEDGE OF GALACTIC SPECIES TO PUT ALL THE STICKERS IN THE CORRECT PLACES.

? B

SPECIES: Bith
HOMEWORLD: Clak'dor VII
SIZE: 1.5m tall
EYE COLOUR: Brown

This band is led by a master of the Kloo horn and Gasan string drum. He is a gambler who often loses the band's earnings (and sometimes their instruments) in games of sabacc. The band instruments include a Dorenian Beshniquel or Fizzz, fanfars, a bandfill with horn bells and the difficult ommni box.

? C

SPECIES: Ithorian
HOMEWORLD: Ithor
SIZE: 1.95m tall
VEHICLE: Tafanda Bay Cityship
WEAPON: Blaster

This alien is a secret agent for the Alliance. Members of his species are generally peaceful farmers and artisans. They are sometimes called Hammerheads. After being exiled from Ithor, he ended up on Tatooine where he helped to shelter Rebel fugitives and passed information to the Alliance.

? E

SPECIES: Devaronian
HOMEWORLD: Devaron
SIZE: 1.8m tall
EYE COLOUR: Brown

This alien Is a devilish-looking spy who became known as the Butcher of Montellian Serat after he destroyed an entire city. On his home planet he was once a cruel army captain who supported the Empire. He has red-tinted skin and two sets of teeth, but is actually not a very good spy.

? F

SPECIES: Human
SIZE: 1.7m tall
EYE COLOUR: Brown
HAIR COLOUR: Black and Grey
WEAPON: SE-14c blaster pistol

Once a promising surgeon, this man's genius turned to madness. He set up a business with a forged medical licence and left many innocent victims maimed or mutilated thanks to his 'creative surgery'. A group of his victims and their families posted a bounty of 1,000,000 credits on his head. He had a scarred face and the death sentence on 12 systems.

HISTORY FILES
BATTLE OF YAVIN

THE BATTLE OF YAVIN WAS THE FIRST MAJOR VICTORY FOR THE REBEL ALLIANCE AGAINST THE EMPIRE. REBEL SPIES HAD STOLEN THE PLANS FOR THE EMPIRE'S NEW WEAPON, THE DEATH STAR. THE PLANS REACHED REBEL HEADQUARTERS ON YAVIN 4, BUT THE EMPIRE WAS CLOSE BEHIND. THERE WERE JUST 30 MINUTES BEFORE THE DEATH STAR WOULD BE CLOSE ENOUGH TO DESTROY YAVIN 4, SO THE REBELS GATHERED A SMALL ATTACK FORCE OF Y-WING AND X-WING STARFIGHTERS.

Battle Strategy

The stolen plans had revealed the one weakness of the Death Star – a small thermal exhaust vent. A Rebel starfighter would have to navigate the Death Star trenches, dodging laser fire from gun towers and TIE fighters, and hit the two-metre-wide thermal exhaust vent with a proton torpedo. This would start a chain reaction and explode the battle station's power core.

Impossible Odds

The Rebels seemed to be fighting a losing battle. Although their X-wing and Y-wing starfighters were able to avoid the turbolasers and they managed to destroy many Imperial TIE fighters, the sheer numbers they were fighting appeared to make the Imperials unbeatable.

EXERCISE
Using the words below, complete this summary of the last moments of the battle.

Luke had to hit the .... to save .... Not trusting the ....'s computer, he switched it off and used the .... as .... had taught him. The ....

hurtled into the ...., causing a .... in the Death Star's main ....

The .... was destroyed and the .... had won their first victory.

....

X-wing	Obi-Wan Kenobi	super weapon	proton torpedoes	chain reaction	Yavin 4
exhaust port	target	Force	reactor	Rebels	

Squadron Formation
The Rebel starfighters were arranged into Red Squadron and Gold Squadron. The pilots flew towards the Death Star in tight wings, with a central starfighter flanked by two wingmen.

Squadron Sacrifice
Gold Squadron's commander and his wingmen sped towards the Death Star trench, while the remaining starfighters distracted the TIE fighters and destroyed countless turbolasers. However, Darth Vader realised the danger and piloted his TIE fighter prototype to defend the trench.

The brave squadron pilots tried to reach the thermal exhaust vent, but twice they failed. Eventually only three X-wings remained, including Luke Skywalker.

Unexpected Heroes
Luke sped into the Death Star trench as the Death Star prepared to fire. There were only a few minutes left. At first Luke used the X-wing's targeting computer to lead him towards the exhaust port, but Darth Vader's TIE prototype was close on his tail.

It looked as if the Rebels would be defeated, but suddenly the *Millennium Falcon* swooped towards the Death Star. It fired and Vader's starship spun out of control, leaving Luke free to continue down the trench.

PODRACER

1

2

3

4
A HUTT GANGSTER
GIVES YOU
A NASTY LOOK.
MISS A TURN.

5

6

7

24
YOU OVERTAKE
ANOTHER
PODRACER.
GO TWO SPACES

23

25

26

32

31

30

29

28

27

33

34

35
A TUSKEN
RAIDER TAKES
A SHOT AT YOU.
GO TWO
SPACES BACK.

36

37

38
YOU SHOW OFF
YOUR AMAZING
PILOTING SKILLS.
HAVE ANOTHER
TURN.

39

40

THE ALIENS OF MOS EISLEY CANTINA: PAGE 32

MYO

MUFTAK

FIGRIN D'AN AND THE MODAL NODES
(ALSO KNOWN AS THE CANTINA BAND)

MOMAW NADON

LABRIA

DR EVAZAN

 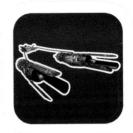  

1 2 3

4 5 6

7 8 9 10

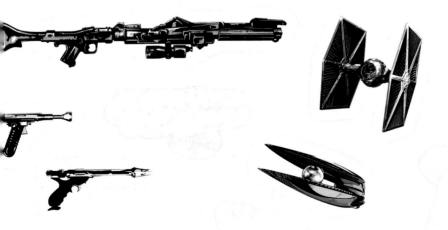

A GAME FOR TWO OR MORE PLAYERS. YOU WILL NEED A MARKER FOR EACH PLAYER AND A DICE. MAKE YOUR MARKERS BY PLACING A STICKER ON A PIECE OF THICK CARD. CUT AROUND THE SHAPE TO MAKE YOUR MARKER. THE AIM OF THE GAME IS TO WIN THE RACE BY REACHING THE END OF THE TRACK.

1. THE FIRST PLAYER TO ROLL A 1 OR A 6 STARTS THE GAME.
2. ROLL THE DICE AGAIN AND MOVE YOUR MARKER ALONG THE NUMBER OF SQUARES SHOWN ON THE DICE.
3. KEEP ROLLING THE DICE AND MOVING YOUR MARKER ALONG THE BOARD. FOLLOW THE INSTRUCTIONS IN THE SQUARES.
4. YOU MUST THROW THE CORRECT NUMBER WITH YOUR DICE TO LAND ON THE FINAL SQUARE AND WIN THE GAME.

8

9 YOU BREAK A SPEED RECORD. GO FORWARD THREE SPACES.

10   **11**   **12**   **13**   **14**

15 SEBULBA KNOCKS YOU OFF COURSE. MISS A TURN.

22   **21**   **20**   **19**   **18**   **17**   **16**

44

45 YOU TAKE THE WRONG TURNING. CHANGE MARKER POSMONS WITH THE PLAYER WHO SPOKE LAST.

46   **47**   **48**   **49**

43

50

41   **42**

THE GALACTIC ADVENTURES OF...

FILL IN YOUR NAME AND RECORD THE MOST EXCITING AND MEMORABLE EVENTS OF THE SUMMER IN THIS EXCLUSIVE DATA LOG.

MY NAME

....

DIARY

MOST HEROIC MOMENT OF 2009:

TOP JEDI FRIENDS:

1.

2.

3.

DIARY

DIARY

DIARY

GREATEST HOPE:

GREATEST FEAR:

WEAKNESSES:

1.

2.

3.

STRENGTHS:

1.

2.

3.

BEST SPORTING MOMENT:

FAVOURITE ACTIVITY:

41

HISTORY FILES
BATTLE OF HOTH

THE BATTLE OF HOTH WAS ONE OF THE REBEL ALLIANCE'S WORST DEFEATS. AFTER THEIR VICTORY AT THE BATTLE OF YAVIN, THE ALLIANCE HAD TO KEEP CHANGING ITS COMMAND BASE TO AVOID IMPERIAL FORCES. HOTH, A REMOTE, FROZEN PLANET, SEEMED A GOOD HIDING PLACE. BUT THEY HADN'T EVEN FINISHED BUILDING THE BASE WHEN AN IMPERIAL PROBE DROID FOUND THEM. DARTH VADER WAS INFORMED, AND THE LEGIONS OF THE MIGHTY GALACTIC EMPIRE SPED TOWARDS THE REBELS..

Battle Strategy

The Imperial forces were led by General Maximilian Veers, a brilliant tactical soldier. His aim was to surprise the Alliance base and capture all the Rebels. The Alliance leader was General Carlist Rieekan. Rieekan was determined to take the Rebels to safety. As soon as he knew that they were under attack, he gave the order to prepare the Rebel transports for evacuation. He also sent Rogue Squadron out to distract and delay the Imperial forces.

Tactical Error

Admiral Ozzel made a foolish blunder at the start of the Imperial attack. He emerged from hyperspace too close to the Hoth system, which warned the Rebels about the fleet's approach.

The Rebels needed all the warning and time they could get. Imperial Star Destroyers quickly moved into position, and enormous AT-AT walkers and legions of snowtroopers moved against the base.

Many Rebel .... escaped ...., but the Rebels suffered heavy .... For the rest of the Galactic ...., their .... were very low. Now, more than ever before, every single member of the .... was vital to their success.
....

Civil War	transports	casualties
Rebel Alliance	Hoth	numbers

REBEL SNOWSPEEDER
TYPE: Modified T-47 airspeeder
SIZE: 5.3m long
TOP SPEED: 1,100 kph
CREW: 2
WEAPONS: Double laser cannon, power harpoon
FLIGHT CEILING: 175km

Blizzard Force

As soon as he entered the Hoth system, Veers sent several AT-AT landing barges and Imperial transports to attack the Alliance troops. The AT-AT squad, known as Blizzard Force, was made up of several AT-AT walkers, each commanded by an Imperial officer. AT-ST walkers protected the AT-ATs as they marched towards the Rebel base.

Stalling Techniques

Rogue Squadron flew modified T-47 airspeeders to stall the AT-ATs. These snowspeeders flew in a loose delta formation to draw AT-AT fire away from the Rebel ground troops.

The snowspeeders' laser cannons could not harm the AT-ATs, so Wedge Antilles tried a daring tactic. He used his airspeeder's harpoon and tow cable to entangle an AT-AT's legs, making it fall it to the ground, helpless.

Escape

As Rogue Squadron battled Blizzard Force, the Rebel transports began their escape. At first, the transports launched one by one. As each one took off, anion cannon gave them covering fire, slamming into the Imperial Star Destroyers that were trying to trap them on the planet. However, as the AT-ATs came closer and closer, the Rebels were forced to launch the transports in pairs.

ARCHIVE FILES
PLANET PROFILES: NABOO

NABOO IS COVERED BY THICK SWAMPS, ROLLING PLAINS AND GREEN HILLS. IT IS HOME TO TWO MAJOR SPECIES – THE NABOO AND THE GUNGANS. THE NABOO LIVE IN BEAUTIFUL CITIES SUCH AS THEED, WHILE THE GUNGANS LIVE IN EXOTIC BUBBLE CITIES HIDDEN IN LAKES AND SWAMPS. NABOO IS ALSO HOME TO A WIDE VARIETY OF ANIMALS, FROM THE GENTLE SHAAK TO THE DEADLY COLO SLAWFISH.

Pronunciation: nah-BOO
Size: 12,120km diameter
Distance from core: 34,000 light years
Suns: 1
Moons: 3
Surface water: 85%
Composition: Honeycomb rock and plasma
Climate: Temperate
Terrain: Swamps, plains, hills and cities

Native Species: Naboo, Gungans, kaadu, falumpasets, fambaas, motts, nunas, peko pekos, ikopi, shaaks, colo claw fish, sando aqua monsters, opee sea killers, pikobis, nola grass, rootjigger, fanned rawl, bolle bol, flewt, horned krevol, flaark, leaf nisp, luhg worm, capper spineflap, flewt, pentapus, gnort, hermit spider, razor crab, great grass plains tusk cat
Population: 1.2 billion
Places of Interest: Otoh Gunga, Theed, Port Landien Perfumery, Keren Kwilaan Starport, Lake Varum, Ohma-D'un, Camp Four, Camp Six, Harte Secur, Spinnaker, Lors, Moenia, Kaadara

At the core of the planet is a gigantic honeycomb structure surrounding massive, solid rocks. The planet is filled with caves and tunnels, some of which actually cross through the very centre.

The first human colony on the planet was founded nearly 4,000 years before the Battle of Naboo. The humans soon met the Gungans, the planet's native species. The two species did not trust each other, so the humans kept to the grassy plains and ocean coastlines, rarely entering Gungan territory.

REPUBLIC CRUISER
TYPE: *Consular*-class space cruiser
AFFILIATION: Jedi
SIZE: 115m long
WEAPONS: None

SITH INFILTRATOR
TYPE: Infiltrator star courier
AFFILIATION: Sith
SIZE: 26.5m long
WEAPONS: Laser cannons, cloaking device

SLAVE I
TYPE: Pursuit vessel
AFFILIATION: Bounty hunter
SIZE: 21.5m long
WEAPONS: Laser cannons, concealed projectile launchers,
ion cannons, tractor beam

SUPER STAR DESTROYER
TYPE: Star Dreadnaught
AFFILIATION: Empire
SIZE: 19,000m
WEAPONS: Turbolasers, ion cannons

TIE AVENGER
TYPE: Advanced space superiority starfighter
AFFILIATION: Empire
SIZE: 10m long
WEAPONS: Laser cannons, warhead launchers

TIE BOMBER
TYPE: Starfighter
AFFILIATION: Empire
SIZE: 7.8m long
WEAPONS: Laser cannons, proton bombs

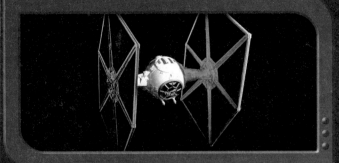

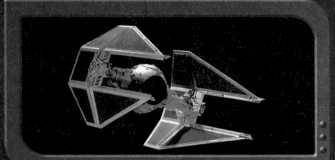

TIE FIGHTER
TYPE: Starfighter
AFFILIATION: Empire
SIZE: 6.3m long
WEAPONS: Laser cannons

TIE INTERCEPTOR
TYPE: Space superiority fighter
AFFILIATION: Empire
SIZE: 9.6m long
WEAPONS: Laser cannons

TRADE FEDERATION CRUISER
TYPE: Carrier/destroyer (*Providence*-class)
AFFILIATION: Trade Federation
SIZE: 1,088m long
WEAPONS: Quad turbolaser turrets, dual laser cannons, ion cannons, point-defence ion cannons, proton torpedo tubes

TRADE FEDERATION LANDING SHIP
TYPE: Landing Ship
AFFILIATION: Trade Federation
SIZE: 370m wide
WEAPONS: Laser cannons

X-WING STARFIGHTER
TYPE: Starfighter
AFFILIATION: Rebel Alliance
SIZE: 12.5m long
WEAPONS: Laser cannons, proton torpedoes

VEHICLE DESIGN STATION

FOLLOW THE STEPS BELOW TO LEARN HOW TO DRAW ONE OF THE MOST FAMOUS VEHICLE DESIGNS IN THE GALAXY.

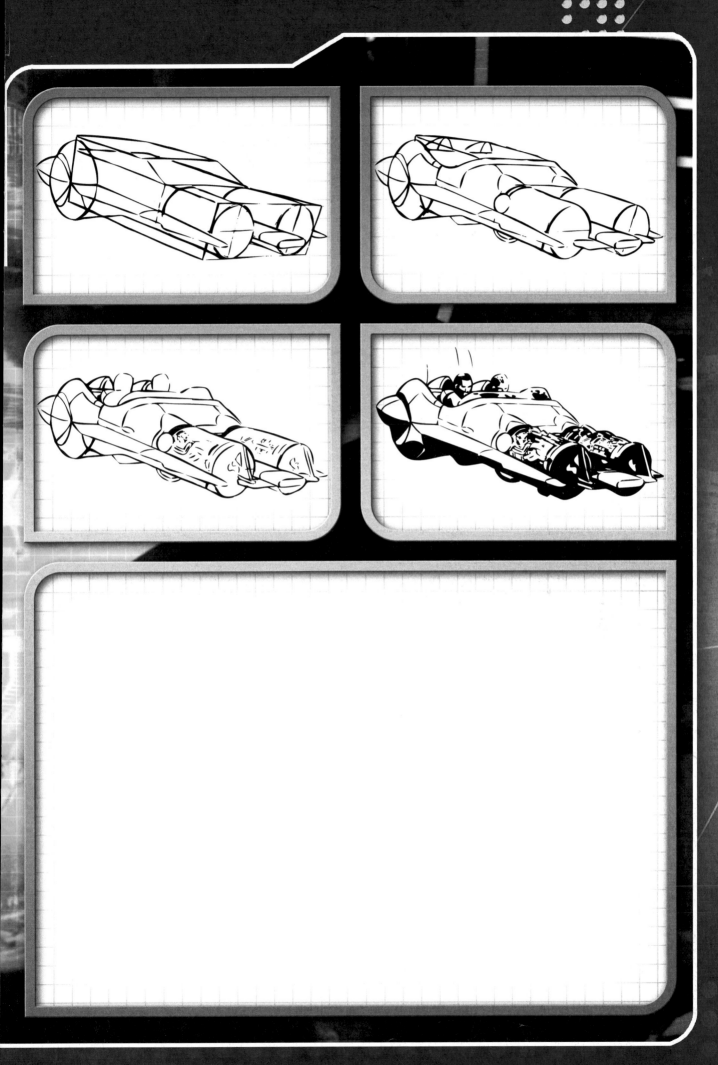

WHAT'S MY NAME?

1.
"I collect the lightsabers of the Jedi I kill."

2.
"I brought up my stepbrother's son."

3.
"I have a purple lightsaber."

4.
"I accompany Han Solo on smuggling missions."

EACH OF THESE STATEMENTS BELONGS TO THE PORTRAIT OF A FAMOUS FACE FROM HISTORY, NOW HANGING IN THE GALACTIC MUSEUM. CAN YOU IDENTIFY EACH ONE? AS YOU NAME THEM, FIND THE RIGHT STICKER AND PUT IT IN THE CORRECT FRAME.

5.
"Meesa berry clumsy."

6.
"I am a bounty hunter, just like my father."

7.
"I asked the Jedi Council to let me train Anakin Skywalker, but they refused."

8.
"When 900 years old you reach, look as good you will not."

DARTH VADER'S

KILLING THE YOUNGLINGS IN THE JEDI TEMPLE
Darth Vader stormed the Jedi Temple with his elite clone trooper special forces and cut down the terrified Jedi younglings.

SLAUGHTERING THE TUSKEN RAIDERS
Anakin slaughtered every Tusken man, woman and child of the tribe that killed his mother.

CUTTING OFF LUKE'S HAND
During a ferocious lightsaber battle, Vader cut off his son's hand. He tried to turn him to the dark side, but Luke preferred death to treachery. He was rescued by Princess Leia.

TORTURING PRINCESS LEIA
When Darth Vader captured Princess Leia, Grand Moff Tarkin ordered him to torture her until she revealed the location of the hidden Rebel base. Vader obeyed, not knowing that he was torturing his own daughter.

DARKEST HOUR

ANAKIN SKYWALKER IS PERHAPS THE MOST FAMOUS JEDI OF ALL TIME — HE WAS THE CHOSEN ONE WHO TURNED TO THE DARK SIDE. HE WAS RESPONSIBLE FOR MANY HORRORS, BUT WHAT DO YOU THINK WAS HIS WORST MOMENT?

LOOK AT THESE TEN DEEDS AND PUT THEM IN ORDER OF EVILNESS. WHICH DO YOU RATE AS NUMBER ONE — HIS MOST TERRIBLE ACT OF ALL TIME? USE THE STICKERS TO RANK THE DEEDS.

FORCE-CHOKING PADMÉ
Anakin's wife refused to believe that he had turned to the dark side, and she went looking for him, trusting in his love for her. Believing that she had betrayed him, Anakin used the Force to choke her. Padmé's heart was broken, and she died soon afterwards.

ASSISTING IN THE DEATH OF MACE WINDU
When Mace Windu duelled with the Emperor, Anakin cut off the Jedi Master's hand, enabling Palpatine to kill him.

DUELLING WITH OBI-WAN
When Obi-Wan tried to draw Anakin back to the light side, they had a terrible duel that led to Anakin's grievous wounds. Many years later they duelled again, and this time Anakin killed the man who had once been like a brother to him.

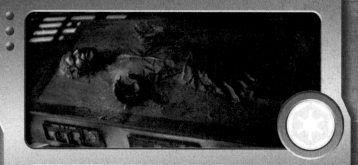

FREEZING HAN SOLO IN CARBONITE
Darth Vader had a carbon-freezing chamber converted to function on humans. He tested it on Han Solo. Han survived the process but remained imprisoned in carbonite for over a year.

KILLING THE SEPARATIST LEADERS
In a war room on Mustafar, the Separatists gathered to await Darth Vader at the end of the Clone Wars. When he arrived, he used the Force to close all the exits and then slaughtered the Separatists.

TAKING LUKE TO MEET THE EMPEROR
Luke gave himself up to Darth Vader, desperate to reach the last spark of good that he believed was still inside his father. But Vader took him to Emperor Palpatine's throne room aboard the Death Star and allowed the Emperor to torment him.

ARCHIVE FILES
PLANET PROFILES: GEONOSIS

GEONOSIANS ARE INSECTOIDS THAT LIVE IN TOWERING SPIRE-HIVES AND VALUE THEIR PRIVACY. THESE ARE SO CAREFULLY MADE THAT THEY LOOK AS IF THEY ARE PART OF THE PLANET'S SURFACE.

Pronunciation: gee-oe-NOE-siss
Size: 11,370 km diameter
Distance from core: 43,000 light years
Suns: 1
Moons: 4 major; 11 minor
Surface water: 5%

Composition: Diminutive molten core with rocky mantle
Climate: Dry
Terrain: Rock, desert
Native Species: Geonosians, massiffs, porlceetin, windrail, hydra
Population: 100 billion
Places of Interest: Stalgasin Hive, Execution Arena, Droid Factory, Command Centre, Ebon Sea, N'rakti Lava Fields

Geonosis is the second of five rocky worlds that orbit a yellow sun in a dangerous sector of the Outer Rim. It is a hard, unwelcoming world. The planet suffers from many asteroid showers. Flash floods and groundwater eruptions are common. The rocks and sky are tinted red, and the creatures that live there are well equipped to survive in difficult conditions. Radiation storms sometimes blast the surface, and a dense fog gives the day a gloomy, night-like appearance.

Geonosis is the closest inhabited planet to Tatooine, and it is full of large factories for the production of droids and weapons. The rings that orbit Geonosis provide raw materials for their mysterious manufacturing processes. However, corporate spies sometimes hide inside the rings, trying to learn Geonosian secrets.

FAMASY TEAM

LUKE SKYWALKER WAS A HERO OF THE REBEL ALLIANCE, BUT ONE OF HIS GREATEST STRENGTHS WAS THE TEAM OF FRIENDS WHO SUPPORTED HIM. WHO WOULD YOU CHOOSE TO BE ON YOUR TEAM IF YOU HAD TO TRAVEL THROUGH THE GALAXY AND FIGHT EVIL? USE PHOTOS OF YOUR FAMILY AND FRIENDS OR CUT IMAGES FROM MAGAZINES. GET INSPIRATION FROM THE BLUEPRINT TEMPLATES AND INCORPORATE STICKERS TO BUILD YOUR OWN FANTASY TEAM.

YOU
Do you have what it takes to be a hero?

BEST FRIEND
Who will stand by your side through all your adventures?

WISE ADVISOR
Who can you always turn to for help and guidance?

WEAPON
Remember, keep it simple and elegant, just like a lightsaber.

TRANSPORT
Will you need a spaceship? How will you travel on the planet's surface?

WILD CARD
Who or what else will join you on your trip? A super-intelligent pet or a beautiful princess?

FAVOURITE JEDI

THERE ARE MANY EXCITING STORIES DESCRIBING THE ADVENTURES OF THE JEDI KNIGHTS. HERE ARE SOME OF THE MOST MEMORABLE. DO YOU REMEMBER THEM ALL?

POSSIBLY the most dangerous adventure that Obi-Wan Kenobi ever had took him to the cruel world of Geonosis, where he became part of a barbaric game. Together with his Padawan, Anakin Skywalker, and Senator Amidala, Obi-Wan looked into the jaws of death when the Geonosians set three hideous beasts on them.

THIS wampa was nearly the end of Luke Skywalker. He escaped it on the frozen world of Hoth, only to fall unconscious into the snow. Luckily, his friend Han Solo had already set out to find him. The two men sheltered all night long using the body of a dead tauntaun, and survived to face an Imperial attack.

MASTER Yoda was one of the most skilled lightsaber duellists the galaxy has ever known. His connection with the Force was unsurpassed, and his speed and agility in battle were a match for Count Dooku's elegant precision. Their fierce battle on Geonosis was a dazzling display of skill on both sides, but ultimately Count Dooku knew that he could not win.

MOMENTS

ANOTHER amazing moment in the Jedi annals happened when Obi-Wan Kenobi faced the Sith apprentice Darth Maul. Obi-Wan's beloved Master had just been slain, but despite his grief he knew that this tattooed creature had to be stopped. Their duel has gone down in history as one of the most electrifying of all time.

LUKE Skywalker was looking for a wise Jedi Master when he crash landed in a swamp. The strange, green creature that he met there seemed foolish and irritating at first. But this was Yoda, the wisest of all Jedi Masters, and it was his task to train the impulsive young Skywalker. At first Luke doubted his own abilities, but Master Yoda taught him how powerful the Force could be.

WHEN Jabba the Hutt took Luke Skywalker and his friends to the Pit of Carkoon, he intended to feed them to the Sarlacc. Luke gave the hideous gangster a chance to live in peace, but he refused. What followed was one of the most awe-inspiring rescues and escapes ever seen in the history of the galaxy. Within a few short minutes, Jabba was dead, his followers were thrown into the pit, and Luke and his friends were free.

WHICH IS YOUR TOP JEDI MOMENT? PUT THESE EVENTS IN ORDER OF YOUR FAVOURITES BY WRITING IN THE SPACES PROVIDED.

HISTORY FILES
BATTLE OF ENDOR

THE BATTLE OF ENDOR HAS GONE DOWN IN HISTORY AS THE MOST DECISIVE FIGHT OF THE GALACTIC CIVIL WAR. IT MARKED THE BIRTH OF THE NEW REPUBLIC WITH THE DESTRUCTION OF THE SECOND DEATH STAR AND THE DEATHS OF DARTH VADER AND EMPEROR PALPATINE.

News reached the Rebels that the Emperor was building a second even more powerful Death Star and that he would be on board the Death Star himself. The Rebels planned to destroy the Death Star, but they didn't guess the terrible truth. The Emperor had planted this information as a trap to catch them.

The Rebels' Plan

The second Death Star was in orbit around the forest moon of Endor. A shield generator on Endor created a defensive screen around the Death Star, protecting it from attack. First the Rebels had to turn off the shield generator. Then their fleet could launch a surprise attack on the Death Star. The timing had to be perfect.

Admiral Ackbar gathered the Alliance fleet around the planet Sullust, while a special strike team was sent ahead to sabotage the shield generator. The team was led by Han Solo and included Luke Skywalker, Princess Leia, Chewbacca, R2-D2, C-3PO and a squad of Rebel commandos. Their job was vital to the success of the battle. They had to turn off the shield by the time the Rebel fleet emerged from hyperspace so that the surprise attack could begin.

The Emperor's Plan

The Emperor knew all about the Rebels' plan. A full legion of stormtroopers was waiting inside the shield generator to capture the Rebel strike team. When the Rebel fleet arrived, they would find the protective shield still in place. TIE fighters would demolish the outnumbered Rebel starfighters. Next, the Death Star's fully operational superlaser would vaporise all of the Alliance's control ships. The Emperor intended to destroy the Rebels once and for all.

EXERCISE
Using the words opposite, complete this summary of the Battle of Endor.

Without the ...., the .... weakened and ....were

scattered. The .... was free to begin building the ....

Balance had come to the .... at last.

New Republic
Emperor
dark side
Force
Imperial forces
Rebel Alliance

Captured

When Han and his team reached the shield generator on Endor, they discovered a squad of the Empire's finest troops waiting for them. The Rebels were surrounded with no way of warning their fleet.

Outnumbered

In the skies above Endor, the Rebel fleet exited hyperspace near the Death Star. Lando Calrissian, aboard the *Millennium Falcon*, led the starfighter attack as Gold Leader.

As soon as Admiral Ackbar realised that the Death Star's shield was still active, he wanted to call off the attack, but Lando had faith that Han would not let them down and he persuaded the Admiral to continue. They were met by a massive fleet of TIE craft, including standard fighters and interceptors.

Fully Operational

To their horror, the Alliance fleet discovered that the Death Star's superlaser was in full working order. It destroyed one Mon Cal cruiser and was ready to fire again, when Lando suggested a clever tactic. If they flew close to the Imperial Star Destroyer; the Death Star wouldn't fire without risking destroying its own fleet.

Tiny Heroes

On Endor, the Ewoks rescued Han and his team. They outwitted the clumsy AT-STs and used traps to crash speeder bikes. Han managed to destroy the shield generator. Now it was up to the fleet to win the battle in the sky.

The Beginning of the End

As soon as the shield dropped, Lando and Wedge Antilles flew into the Death Star and attacked the main reactor core. The resulting chain reaction destroyed the Death Star and also killed the Emperor.

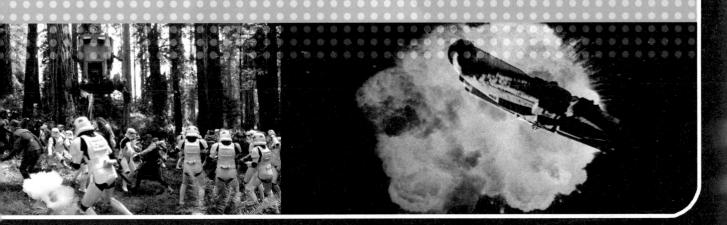

DROID DESIGN STATION

SUPER BATTLE DROID

SIZE: 1.91m tall
WEAPONS: Built-in wrist blaster, wrist launcher
SUBTYPE: Droid (class 4)

DROID DESIGN REQUIRES IMAGINATION, INTELLIGENCE AND A STEADY HAND. USE THIS GRID DESIGN BLUEPRINT OF A SUPER BATTLE DROID TO CREATE YOUR OWN VERSION OF THE POWERFUL AND TIRELESS SOLDIER.

SUPER BATTLE DROID

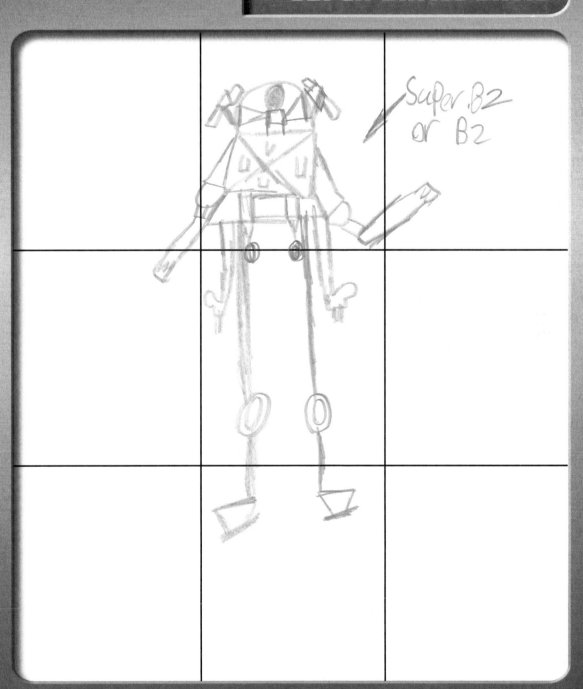

Super.B2 or B2

ANSWERS

PAGE 10

```
Q W H E R T Y U R I O E P A S D F G C
A S D T F G H A J K L m L Z X C V O I
F V B N I N T m Q A Z P W S X E R D L
D E C R F S V B G T Y I V B G U T Y B
Y H T n H m J P I H S R A T S U I O U
L P m T n B V m C X Z E A C S D A F P
G H A J K L P O U I U Y A T R D E W E
Q E m A S D F G H S J n K L O P O C R
D O I E R O T Y S n T P O V I U Y L E
E W R Q L K B J H G F A D S A A Z O X
X C R V B n B I G R V S F D D I R n U
P O E U Y O S A W E R V X A n D m E J
Q W T E R C T V U A I O P J R E G S D
T T U H G L G F A R n A X O E J A D P
B V O O B A R X D O E L I L G T E D C
R T Y U I F O P L K J O H G E F D S A
T n m D S E R T Y U S J A F D C C V W
I J B F E S Z X D F T Y U V I O R L n
S K Y W A L K E R U R V S F Q W E O S
Z X C G H J U I O W E R T Y U I O P F
```

PAGE 11

1. TRUE	**8.** TRUE	**15.** TRUE
2. TRUE	**9.** FALSE	**16.** FALSE
3. TRUE	**10.** FALSE	**17.** FALSE
4. FALSE	**11.** TRUE	**18.** TRUE
5. TRUE	**12.** FALSE	**19.** FALSE
6. TRUE	**13.** FALSE	**20.** FALSE
7. FALSE	**14.** TRUE	

PAGE 16/17

1. Nute Gunray and his lieutenant, Rune Haako, were taken into Republic custody.

2. The Gungans and Naboo formed a lasting peace.

3. Anakin Skywalker became Obi-Wan Kenobi's Padawan.

PAGE 24/25

The Battle of Geonosis resulted in the deaths of many Jedi and legions of clone troopers. Even though the Republic won the battle, they made the Separatists more determined to continue. The Clone Wars had begun.

PAGE 30/31

1. a. Chewbacca, Wookiee
   b. Jar Jar Binks, Gungan
   c. Wicket W Warwick, Ewok

2. False

3. None – he used the Force.

4. Because his aunt and uncle were killed by stormtroopers.

5. Anakin Skywalker

6. Geonosis

7. Shmi Skywalker

8. Because he wanted to learn how to stop death and save Padmé's life.

9. Kamino

10. Darth Maul

11. When he fought Mace Windu.

12. Forest moon of Endor

13. Chancellor Palpatine

14. "There is still good in him."

15. Because he sensed that his friends were in danger.

16. Zam Wesell

17. Mos Eisley Cantina

18. Get married

19. a. General Grievous Guard
   b. Darth Vader
   c. Darth Maul

20. ". . . be with you."

PAGE 34/35

Luke had to hit the target to save Yavin 4. Not trusting the X-wing's computer, he switched it off and used the Force as Obi-Wan Kenobi had taught him. The proton torpedoes hurtled into the exhaust port, causing a chain reaction in the Death Star's main reactor. The super weapon was destroyed and the Rebels had won their first victory.

PAGE 42/43

Many Rebel transports escaped Hoth, but the Rebels suffered heavy casualties. For the rest of the Galactic Civil War, their numbers were very low. Now, more than ever before, every single member of the Rebel Alliance was vital to their success.

PAGE 50/51

1. General Grievous

2. Owen Lars

3. Mace Windu

4. Chewbacca

5. Jar Jar Binks

6. Boba Fett

7. Qui-Gon Jinn

8. Master Yoda

PAGE 62/63

Without the Emperor, the dark side weakened and Imperial forces were scattered. The Rebel Alliance was free to begin building the New Republic. Balance had come to the Force at last.